EEYORE HAS
A BIRTHDAY

A. A. Milne

Eeyore Has a Birthday

adapted by Stephen Krensky

with decorations by Ernest H. Shepard

Puffin Books

PUFFIN BOOKS
Published by the Penguin Group
Penguin Putnam Books for Young Readers, 345 Hudson Street, New York, New York 10014, U.S.A.
Penguin Books Ltd, 27 Wrights Lane, London W8 5TZ, England
Penguin Books Australia Ltd, Ringwood, Victoria, Australia
Penguin Books Canada Ltd, 10 Alcorn Avenue, Toronto, Ontario, Canada M4V 3B2
Penguin Books (N.Z.) Ltd, 182-190 Wairau Road, Auckland 10, New Zealand

Penguin Books Ltd, Registered Offices: Harmondsworth, Middlesex, England

First published in the United States of America by Dutton Children's Books and Puffin Books,
divisions of Penguin Putnam Books for Young Readers, 2001

1 3 5 7 9 10 8 6 4 2

LIBRARY OF CONGRESS CATALOGING-IN-PUBLICATION DATA
Krensky, Stephen.
Eeyore has a birthday / A.A. Milne; adapted by Stephen Krensky; with decorations by
Ernest H. Shepard.—1st ed.
p. cm
Summary: Because Eeyore feels ignored on his birthday, Pooh and
Piglet attempt to provide a proper celebration.
ISBN 0-525-46764-5 (hardcover)—ISBN 0-14-230042-X (pbk.)
[1. Birthdays—Fiction. 2. Toys—Fiction. 3. Teddy bears—Fiction. 4. Friendship—Fiction.] I.
Shepard, Ernest H. (Ernest Howard), 1879-1976, ill. II. Milne, A. A. (Alan Alexander), 1882-1956. III. Title.
PZ7.K883 Ee 2001
[E]—dc21 2001023923

Puffin Easy-to-Read ISBN 0-14-230042-X
Puffin® and Easy-to-Read® are registered trademarks of Penguin Putnam Inc.

Printed in China

Reading Level 1.8

Contents

1

EEYORE REVEALS
A SECRET

Eeyore, the old grey Donkey,

stood by the side of the stream.

He looked at himself in the water.

"Pathetic," he said.

"That's what it is.

Pathetic."

He turned and walked away slowly

down the stream.

There was a crackling noise

in the bracken behind him,

and out came Winnie-the-Pooh.

"Good morning, Eeyore," said Pooh.

"Good morning, Pooh Bear," said Eeyore.

"If it *is* a good morning,

which I doubt."

"Why, what's the matter?" asked Pooh.

Eeyore sighed.

"Nothing, Pooh Bear, nothing," he said.

"We can't all, and some of us don't.

That's all there is to it."

"Oh," said Pooh.

He sat down on a large stone

and tried to think this out.

It sounded to him like a riddle.

Pooh was never much good at riddles,

being a Bear of Very Little Brain.

So he sang *Cottleston Pie* instead.

Cottleston, Cottleston, Cottleston Pie,

A fly can't bird, but a bird can fly.

Ask me a riddle and I reply:

"Cottleston, Cottleston, Cottleston Pie."

"That's right," said Eeyore.

"Sing. Enjoy yourself."

"You seem so sad, Eeyore," said Pooh.

"Sad?" said Eeyore. "Why should I be sad?

It's my birthday,

the happiest day of the year."

"Your birthday?" said Pooh in great surprise.

"Of course," said Eeyore.

"Look at all the presents.

Look at the birthday cake.

Candles and pink sugar."

Pooh looked—

first to the right

and then to the left.

"Presents?" said Pooh.

"Birthday cake? Where?"

"Can't you see them?" asked Eeyore.

"No," said Pooh.

"Neither can I," said Eeyore.

"Joke. Ha ha!"

This was too much for Pooh.

"Stay there!" he called to Eeyore,

and ran home as fast as he could.

He must get poor Eeyore a present at once.

Outside his house

Pooh found his friend Piglet,

jumping up and down

trying to reach the knocker.

"Hallo, Piglet," said Pooh.

"Hallo, Pooh," said Piglet.

"I was trying to reach the knocker."

"Let me do it for you," said Pooh kindly.

He reached up and knocked

at the door.

"I have just seen Eeyore.

It's his birthday.

Nobody has taken any notice of it,

and he's very gloomy....

Whoever lives here

is taking a long time to answer."

"But Pooh," said Piglet,

"it's your own house."

"Oh," said Pooh. "So it is.

Let's go in."

2

POOH HAS A GREAT MANY IDEAS

The first thing Pooh did

was to go to the cupboard.

He took down a small pot of honey.

"I'm giving this to Eeyore

as a present," he explained.

"What are *you* going to give?"

"Couldn't I give it, too?" asked Piglet.

"From both of us?" he added.

"No," said Pooh.

"That is not a good plan."

"All right, then," said Piglet,

"I'll give him a balloon.

I've got one left from my party."

Pooh nodded.

"That is just what Eeyore wants

to cheer him up.

Nobody can be uncheered

with a balloon."

So off Piglet went to his house,

and Pooh started back to Eeyore.

It was a warm day.

Pooh hadn't gone more than halfway

when a funny feeling crept over him.

It began at the tip of his nose

and trickled all through him

and out at the soles of his feet.

It was as if somebody inside him were saying,

"Now then, Pooh,

time for a little something."

So he sat down and took the top off

his jar of honey.

"Lucky I brought this with me,"

he thought.

And he began to eat.

"Now let me see," he thought,

taking his last lick

on the inside of the pot.

"Where was I going? Ah, yes, Eeyore."

He got up slowly.

Then suddenly he remembered.

He had eaten Eeyore's birthday present.

"Bother!" said Pooh.

"What shall I do?"

For a little while

he couldn't think of anything.

"Well, it's a very nice pot,

even if there is no honey in it.

If I washed it clean

and got somebody

to write *A Happy Birthday* on it,

Eeyore could keep things in it,

which might be Useful."

As he was just passing

the Hundred Acre Wood,

he went inside to call on Owl,

who lived there.

"Good morning, Owl," said Pooh.

"Good morning, Pooh," said Owl.

"Many happy returns

of Eeyore's birthday," Pooh went on.

"Oh, is that what it is?" asked Owl.

"What are you giving him, Owl?"

"What are *you* giving him, Pooh?"

"I'm giving him a Useful Pot

to Keep Things In."

"Is this it?" asked Owl,

taking the pot from Pooh.

"Yes," said Pooh. "And I wanted

to ask you—"

"Somebody has been

keeping honey in it," said Owl.

"You can keep anything in it," Pooh said.

"It's Very Useful like that."

"You ought to write *A Happy Birthday*

on it," Owl pointed out.

"*That* was what I wanted to ask you,"

said Pooh.

"Because my spelling is wobbly.

Would you write

A Happy Birthday on it for me?"

He washed the pot and dried it,

while Owl wondered how to spell *birthday*.

"Can you read, Pooh?" he asked.

"There is a notice outside my door.

Could you read it?"

"Christopher Robin told me what it said,

and then I could," said Pooh.

Owl nodded.

"Well, I'll tell you what *this* says,

and then you'll be able to."

So Owl wrote:

HIPY PAPY BTHUTHDTH THUTHDA
BTHUTHDY.

"I'm just saying *A Happy Birthday*,"

Owl explained.

"It's a nice long one," said Pooh,

very much impressed.

"Actually," said Owl, "I'm saying

A Very Happy Birthday

with love from Pooh.

It takes a good deal of pencil

to say a long thing like that."

"Oh, I see," said Pooh.

3

PIGLET HURRIES
A LITTLE TOO MUCH

Piglet had gone back to his house

to get Eeyore's balloon.

He held it very tightly

so that it wouldn't blow away.

He ran as fast as he could

to get to Eeyore's.

He was thinking how pleased

Eeyore would be.

He didn't look where he was going.

Suddenly, he put his foot

in a rabbit hole

and fell down flat on his face.

BANG!!!???

Piglet lay there,

wondering what had happened.

At first he thought the whole world

had blown up.

Then he thought perhaps only

the Forest part had.

And then he thought

perhaps only *he* had.

Maybe he was now alone

on the moon or somewhere.

He got up and looked about him.

He was still in the Forest!

"Well, that's funny," he thought.

"I wonder what that bang was.

I couldn't have made such a noise

just falling down.

And where's my balloon?

And what's this small piece

of damp rag doing?"

It was the balloon!

"Oh, dear!" said Piglet.

"Oh, dear, oh, dearie, dearie, dear!

I haven't another balloon.

Perhaps Eeyore doesn't like balloons

so very much."

He trotted on rather sadly

and came to the side of the stream

where Eeyore was.

"Good morning, Eeyore," shouted Piglet.

"Good morning, Little Piglet," said Eeyore.

"If it *is* a good morning,

which I doubt."

"Many happy returns of the day,"

said Piglet.

Eeyore stopped to stare at Piglet.

"Meaning me?" he said.

"Of course, Eeyore!" said Piglet.

"My birthday?" said Eeyore.

"Yes, Eeyore," said Piglet,

"and I've brought you a present.

A balloon."

"A balloon?" said Eeyore.

"One of those big colored things

you blow up?"

"Yes," said Piglet, "but—I'm very sorry,

Eeyore—but when I was running along

to bring it to you, I fell down."

"Dear, dear, how unlucky!" said Eeyore.

"You didn't hurt yourself, Little Piglet?"

"No," said Piglet.

"But I—I—oh, Eeyore,

I burst the balloon!"

There was a very long silence.

"My balloon?" said Eeyore at last.

Piglet nodded.

"My birthday balloon?"

"Yes, Eeyore," said Piglet, sniffing a little.

"Here it is." He gave Eeyore

the small piece of damp rag.

"Is this it?" said Eeyore, a little surprised.

Piglet nodded.

"The balloon?"

Piglet nodded again.

"Thank you, Piglet," said Eeyore.

"What color was this balloon

when it—when it *was* a balloon?"

"Red."

"Red," said Eeyore.

"My favorite color.

And how big was it?"

"About as big as me," said Piglet.

"About as big as Piglet," said Eeyore.

"My favorite size. Well, well."

Piglet didn't know what to say.

4

EEYORE CELEBRATES AT LAST

Piglet heard a shout

from the other side of the river,

and there was Pooh.

"Many happy returns of the day, Eeyore,"

called Pooh, forgetting

he had said it already.

"I've brought you a little present," he added.

"It's a Useful Pot.

And it's got *A Very Happy Birthday*

with love from Pooh written on it.

It's for putting things in."

When Eeyore saw the pot,

he became quite excited.

"Why!" he said. "I believe my balloon

will just go into that pot!"

"Oh, no," said Pooh.

"Balloons are much too big to—"

"Not mine," said Eeyore proudly.

He picked up the balloon

with his teeth

and placed it carefully in the pot.

Then he picked it out

and put it on the ground.

Then he picked it up again

and put it carefully back.

"So it does!" said Pooh.

"It goes in!"

"So it does!" said Piglet.

"And it comes out!"

"It goes in and out like anything,"

Eeyore said.

"I'm very glad," Pooh said happily,

"that I thought of giving you

a Useful Pot to put things in."

"And I'm very glad," said Piglet happily,

"that I thought of giving you Something

to put in a Useful Pot."

But Eeyore wasn't listening.

He was taking the balloon out,

and putting it back again,

as happy as he could be.